Jeepers Creepers

A Monstrous ABC

To Melinda and John F., with love —L. E.

For Mick and Ginny, and all the little monsters next door —D. P.

lmnop

No part of this publication may be reproduced, stored in a retrieval system,
or transmitted in any form or by any means, electronic, mechanical, photocopying,
recording, or otherwise, without written permission of the publisher. For information
regarding permission, write to Chronicle Books, 85 Second Street,
San Francisco, CA 94105.

ISBN 0-439-67618-5

12 11 10 9 8 7 6 5   7 8 9/0

Printed in the U.S.A.   40

First Scholastic printing, October 2004

Book design by Kristen M. Nobles
Typeset in Amigo
The illustrations in this book were rendered in acrylic
and alkyd paints on acrylic painting paper.

Jeepers Creepers

A Monstrous ABC

by Laura Leuck * illustrated by David Parkins

SCHOLASTIC INC.

New York Toronto London Auckland Sydney

Mexico City New Delhi Hong Kong Buenos Aires

Ann has alligator skin.

B

Bud grows toadstools on his chin.

Cody's belly button glows.

D **Drew blows beetles from his nose.**

Ed's hair smells like sauerkraut.

Freddy's two front fangs fell out.

Gert wears crawdads in her ears.

G H

Hal's head often disappears.

Ida's back has slippery scales.

Jane has corkscrew fingernails.

J

Kendra's tail is spiked and strong.

Lucy's tongue is ten feet long.

M

Marilyn has spider legs.

Nelson's neck has bolts and pegs.

O Oliver has vulture wings.

P Peggy has a thumb that stings.

Quentin's eyebrows tend to crawl.

Rob looks like a basketball.

Sid has fifteen purple toes. S

Tommy's red eyes never close.

U

Ursula has lizard lips.

Vicky's horns have neon tips.

W

X

Winifred breathes flames of fire.

Xavier wears tape attire.

Y Yasmine cannot get much smaller.

Z Zelda's tall and getting taller.

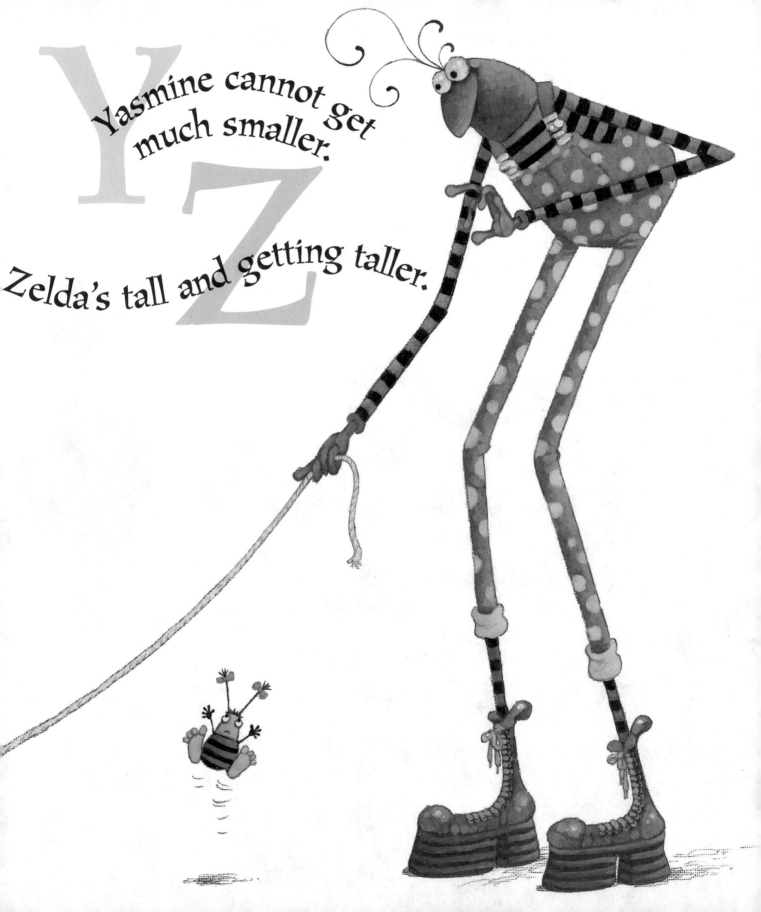

These monster children gather 'round
a book their monster teacher found
of creepy creatures A to Z,
to help them learn their ABCs.

And right before the book is done
they spot a REALLY freaky one—

with blinking eyes, a bumpless chin,
roundish ears and furless skin,
a tiny tongue, a weird hairdo
and such a silly body, too!

They scramble for
a better view.